ICE SKATING
is for me

ICE SKATING
is for me

Lowell A. Dickmeyer
and Lin Rolens

photographs by
Alan Oddie

Lerner Publications Company   Minneapolis

This book has been prepared under the supervision of Ron Priestley, former president of the Ice Skating Institute of America. The authors wish to give him special thanks for his continued advice and support.

The authors also wish to thank Jill Kaysing, Heather and Louis McBurnie, Paul Bergerot, and the management of the Ice Patch in Santa Barbara, California.

Cover photograph and photographs on pages 5, 20, 28, and 39 by Daniel G. Tkash

LIBRARY OF CONGRESS CATALOGING IN PUBLICATION DATA

Dickmeyer, Lowell A.
   Ice skating is for me.

   (A Sports for Me Book)
   SUMMARY: A sister and brother learn the basic skills of ice skating and advance to earn their first skating badge from the Ice Skating Institute of America.

   1. Skating—Juvenile literature. [1. Ice skating] I. Rolens, Lin, joint author. II. Oddie, Alan. III. Title. IV. Series.

GV849.D53   796.9'1   79-20465
ISBN 0-8225-1088-X

Manufactured in the United States of America. Published simultaneously in Canada by J. M. Dent & Sons (Canada) Ltd., Don Mills, Ontario.

International Standard Book Number: 0-8225-1088-X
Library of Congress Catalog Card Number: 79-20465

2 3 4 5 6 7 8 9 10 85 84 83 82 81

Hi! I'm Heather and this is my brother Lewis. One of our favorite things to do is ice skating. We became interested in skating when we saw some Olympic figure skaters on television. Their movements were so powerful and graceful, and they made everything look easy. We knew ice skating was not as easy as they made it look, but we were eager to try it.

We asked our parents if we could take skating lessons. They said we should try ice skating a few times and see if we really liked it. Then, if we were still interested, they would help us pay for classes.

Lewis's friend Paul has been ice skating for almost ten years. He said he would go to the ice rink with us and help us get started. We were very excited the day of our first trip to the rink.

When we got to the rink, we saw a large oval of perfectly flat ice. Many people were skating and they all seemed to be having fun. The air was cool inside and most of the people were wearing slacks

and a sweater or warm shirt. A few girls and women were wearing skating costumes just like the Olympic skaters had worn. I decided that someday I would like to skate in a costume like that.

Lewis and I were both nervous about falling down or looking silly. Paul said we shouldn't be worried. Almost everyone falls down when they first start skating. Even the best skaters fall down when they are learning new moves. He told us that falling on ice is not like falling on pavement. Because you slide when you fall on ice, you are much less likely to hurt yourself.

Paul helped us pick out our skates. He told us that skates should be a half size smaller than our shoe size. He also said that when we rented skates, we should try to get a pair with sharp blades. This makes skating much easier. Paul helped us to put the skates on. We practiced walking on the rubber-padded area around the rink.

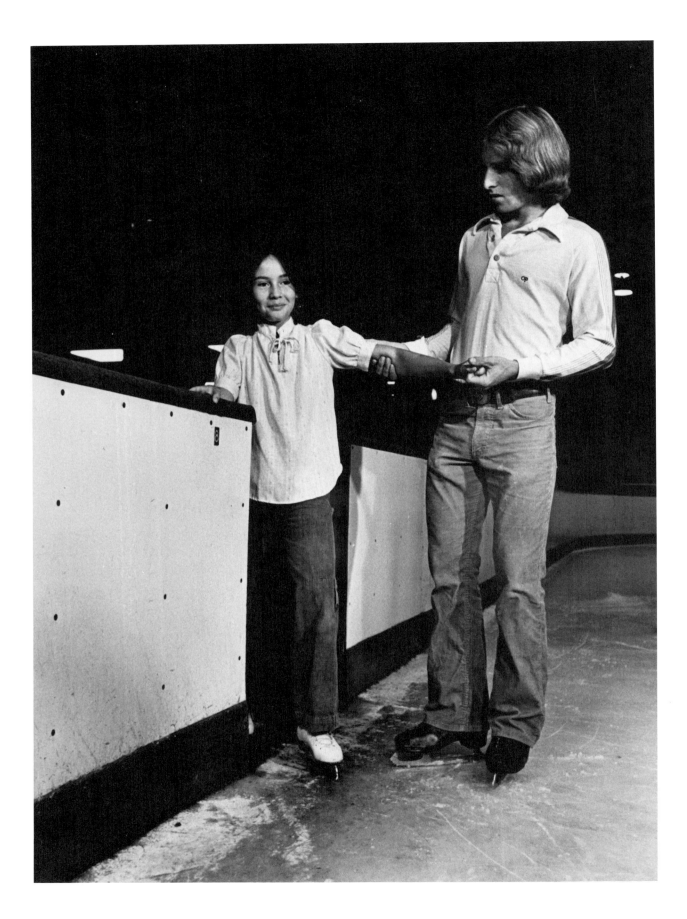

After a few steps we got used to walking on our skates, and Paul led us to the edge of the ice.

Lewis wanted to jump right on, but I was still a little nervous. Paul had us both do the same thing. With our hands on the rail, we each put one foot on the ice and moved it back and forth. Ice is slippery! Then we put the other foot on the ice. We were standing on ice! Still holding onto the rail, we stood first on one foot and then the other, keeping our ankles straight.

Paul told us to keep our knees bent and our backs straight. He also said we should lean forward just a little and try to find a comfortable balance. He reminded us that the main goal in skating is to keep your feet underneath you!

Next, we tried moving on the ice, keeping one hand close to the rail. Holding our heels close together, we turned our toes out a little. We took only two or three very short steps. Then we **glided** on both feet. Gliding is a smooth, flowing movement that is done on the skate blades. Paul told us we should keep our arms out to the side for better balance. He told us to glide on both feet when we started to feel shaky.

There were so many things to remember at first—bending our knees, shifting our weight from one foot to the other, not looking at the ice all the time, keeping our ankles and backs straight, and holding our arms still. After practicing for a little while, we could move more easily without having to think about each separate step.

Finally, Paul led us around the rink one at a time. We kept one hand near the rail and he took the other. He gently pulled us along as we kept our feet parallel. The cool air felt so good and we moved so easily. So this was what ice skating felt like!

By this time Lewis and I were tired. We drank a cup of hot chocolate by the side of the rink while we thought about all the things we had to remember.

Paul took us to the rink several times after that, and we soon became more confident. We told our mother that we really liked skating and thought we were ready for classes. She agreed, and the next afternoon we went to the rink to make the arrangements.

That day we met Jill, who was going to be our teacher. She was really nice and explained many things about skating to us. She told us that as we became better skaters, we could earn special badges that would show how far we had advanced.

Mom decided to buy us skates, so Jill helped each of us pick out a pair. She was very careful since skates that fit well make skating much easier. At first, we thought they felt stiff and a little tight. Jill reminded us that skates must be snug around the heels and ankles to give proper support. Also new skates stretch with use and soon feel comfortable.

This is what our skates look like. They are figure skates. Skaters usually wear figure skates unless they go into hockey or speed skating. Hockey skates do not have **toe picks**, which are the teeth at the front of the blades. Speed skates have the longest blades. They look flat on the bottom and are very thin and light. They don't have toe picks either.

The bottom of the blade on figure skates is slightly curved to make fancy moves and spins possible. Toe picks help skaters do special jumps and spins. They are not often used to stop. Jill said that we are not skating properly when we can hear or feel our toe picks scraping the ice as we skate.

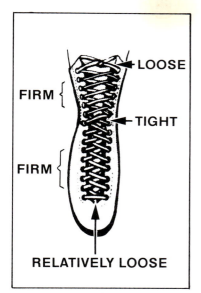

FIRM { LOOSE

TIGHT

FIRM {

RELATIVELY LOOSE

The bottom of each skate blade has a groove down the middle. This means that instead of having flat surfaces to skate on, we have two **edges** for each blade. They are called the **inside** and **outside edges**. They are important because they help control turns and stops, and make many fancy moves possible. The edges also control the direction of our curves.

Jill said it was very important to lace our skates properly, so she showed us how to do it. We left the laces somewhat loose over our toes, so we could still wiggle them. Then we pulled the laces tight over our insteps. Next we laced the hooks all the way up, making the laces less tight as we went along. Jill said we should be able to put two fingers easily into the top of our boots. Then we wrapped the long laces around the top hooks a couple of times. We tied a bow in the front, and tucked the lace ends into the top of our boots so we wouldn't trip over them.

Jill also suggested that we get **skate guards** so we could walk around without hurting the blades. We bought gloves, too, for warmth and for protection in case we fall down. We were all ready for our first class.

The first thing Jill did was teach us how to fall down! She said the most important

thing about falling was that when we felt ourselves start to fall, we should relax and go with it. We should bend our knees and try not to raise our arms. Trying to fight a fall only makes it worse.

Jill had us glide on two feet, bend our knees, and lean slightly forward until we were in a squatting position. Then she told us to sit down on the ice. We were careful not to touch the ice with our hands because accidents on ice can happen if skaters' fingers are run into. Then she showed us how to get up the right way. The correct way to get up from a fall is to kneel on both knees, then on one knee, and then carefully stand up.

Jill also warned us about staying out of other people's way. We should watch for other skaters and we should always skate in the same direction as everyone else.

Jill showed us other important things, too. She said we should not skate stiff-legged, but should always bend our knees

as our blades touch the ice. She told us always to keep our arms stretched out from our sides because skaters use their arms for balance. It is important not to swing our arms, as we do when walking. When we skate, we keep our arms still.

Finally we got to skate. The first thing we learned was **stroking**. This is the method we use to move forward when we skate. Keeping our knees bent, we turned one foot so it made an angle with the heel of the other foot. We pushed against the ice with the inside edge of our back blade. This pushed us forward on our front blade.

As we finished the **push off**, we let our weight change to the front foot.

Then we brought the back foot parallel to our front foot and let ourselves glide on both feet to steady our balance. When we started to slow down, we repeated the stroke, using the other foot to push off.

At first, our strokes were short and choppy. We stayed very close to the rail. But after a while, we started to get the feel of it. As we gained confidence, we learned to stroke from one blade to the other without gliding on two feet between steps. We moved away from the rail and skated with longer glides. It felt wonderful.

Jill said we had done very well for our first lesson. She suggested we come back to practice during the week to build both our strength and our confidence. One of the most important things about skating is the practicing. An Olympic skater may practice six hours every day!

Lewis and I went back to the rink to work on our forward stroking. It was so much fun. When we finished, I went to look at the skating costumes in the shop. I found a beautiful pink one in my size. I decided to start saving my allowance so I could buy it.

I joined Lewis, who was watching the other skaters. The time for public skating was over and the ice had been resurfaced. It looked so shiny and smooth. Advanced skaters were skating in circles. They were doing figure eights. Paul was there, and he explained that the figure eight is two circles the same size that almost touch. The skater glides around the first circle on one

foot, and then changes to the other foot to trace the second circle. Figure eights take much concentration and practice.

To practice figure eights, each skater rents a **patch** of ice that no one else skates on. It is very quiet when a rink is full of skaters practicing their figures. All we could hear was the sound of blades cutting into the ice.

At our next lesson, Jill showed us the **snowplow stops**. A snowplow stop can be done using one or both feet. First we stood holding the rail. We scraped the inside edges of our blades lightly against the ice, causing little flakes of ice to pile up. This is called "making snow." This feeling of making snow was what we should feel when we did the snowplow stops.

Then Jill took us out on the ice and taught us how to do a one-foot snow-plow stop. While gliding in a straight line on both feet, we moved one foot forward. We placed our weight on the back foot, keeping our ankles straight, and our knees bent. We were careful to continue gliding in a straight line. Then we shifted our weight and made snow with the inside edge of our front blade. This slowed us down and brought us to a stop. To help us avoid curving, we brought the opposing arm forward as we slowed down and stopped.

We stayed after our class and practiced
what we had learned that day until the
end of the public session. Then I went
to make sure my skating costume was
still in the shop. When I came out of the
shop, wonderful things were happening on
the ice.

People were skating to music. They were practicing jumps, spins, and spirals. Paul told us the names of the moves. He also told us that there are two parts to figure skating. One is the **compulsory figures**, where everyone traces variations of the figure eight. In compulsory figures, skaters must follow certain patterns and do certain movements.

The other part of figure skating is called **freestyle**. In freestyle, skaters can use their imaginations. They use music to help combine jumps, spins, and many other movements into their programs. A program shows a skater's personality and style of skating.

When Lewis and I went home we told our parents what we had seen. That night I dreamed I was skating my own program in my beautiful pink costume.

In our next class, Jill taught us how to do the **backward swizzle**. This movement is done on two feet. We started with our toes pointed toward each other. We dropped our ankles in a little so we were using the inside edges of our blades. Bending our knees, we let our skates slide backward, away from each other. Then we pulled them together and straightened our knees. We did this again and again, tracing many curves on the ice.

Now we could skate forward and even knew how to move backward! We went skating three more times during the week. At our next class, Jill had us show her each movement we had learned. She said that if we practiced very hard, we could try for the Alpha badge given by the Ice Skating Institute of America (ISIA). The ISIA tests are given in ice rinks throughout the United States to measure how far skaters have advanced. The Alpha badge is for beginning skaters. Skaters who have earned the Alpha badge can enter ISIA competition. How exciting!

Next Jill taught us the **forward cross-over**. First we practiced turning the corners at the ends of the rink on two skates. We skated down the long side of the rink and then glided around the corners on both skates, leaning into the corners. We used our arms like bicycle handlebars. When we turned our arms and shoulders to the left, we curved to the left. We could curve to the right by turning our arms and leaning to the right. After we got the feeling of curving on two feet, we tried the real crossover.

We started by gliding with our skates parallel and leaning into the curve as we placed our arms in the correct positions. Then we lifted our outside skate and brought it forward, past the inside foot. We brought it around the front of the skating foot and stepped down on the inside edge. Then we lifted the other foot, toe first. We kept our weight on the foot we had just put on the ice. I kept forgetting to keep my arms still. Jill said I should be sure to remember my arm positions when I practiced.

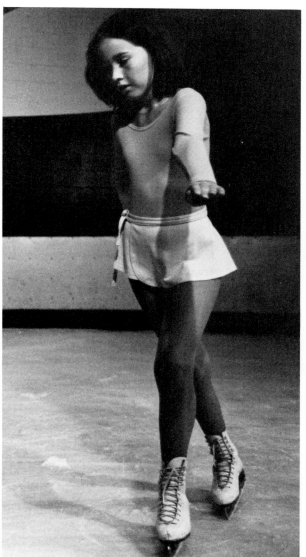

We brought our feet back to the two-foot glide position and tried the move again. In crossovers, the outside foot always crosses around the inside foot as we go around a curve. Crossovers are done only on curves.

Doing crossovers was hard because there was so much to remember. Lewis and I kept working until we started to get the feel of it. Jill gave us help and encouragement. 37

The more we practiced, the more confident we became. Ice skating was getting to be more and more fun. The better we skated, the more eager we were to try new moves.

One day after practice, Jill asked us how confident we felt. We both said we felt very good. I was still a little unsure of my crossovers and Lewis sometimes had trouble with his one-foot snowplow stops. But we knew we could work on these things. Jill explained that in two weeks there would be ISIA badge tests at the rink. She told us to sign up for the Alpha badge test.

We were so excited about the tests that we practiced every day. I counted the money I had saved for my skating costume. I had enough, so the day before our tests I went to the rink to buy it. When I got to the shop, I saw that my skating dress was gone! The clerk said she had sold it only the day before.

The next morning Lewis woke up early and came in to wake me. When I opened my eyes, I saw a box next to my pillow. Mother came into my room and suggested I open it. I was still sleepy but eager to see what was in the box. It was my skating costume! I was so happy!

We got to the rink early and watched some other people take badge tests. Some were advanced and some were beginners, like us. The examiner looked very kind and friendly. He watched carefully as each skater performed the necessary movements for each test. Nearly all of the skaters won their badges but a few people did not skate quite well enough to pass their test.

We were both nervous and excited. Lewis's name was called and he started to skate. I knew Lewis was a little scared, but he skated as if he had all the confidence in the world. He did forward stroking, forward crossovers in each direction, and a one-foot snowplow stop. The examiner didn't say anything, but he smiled and nodded when Lewis finished each move.

He wrote Lewis's scores on a sheet of paper. When the test was finished, Lewis was handed his score sheet—and his badge! He had passed! Lewis had won his first ice skating badge.

I was next. I was nervous too, but I knew I could perform the required movements, and I felt very good in my costume. One by one I did each move. When I finished, I started to skate to the side of the rink but I was called back! I was asked

to do my left crossovers again. I think my hands were shaking, but I nodded and did a new series of left crossovers. I looked up at the examiner, who gave me a big smile. Then he handed me my score sheet—and my badge.

Both Lewis and I had passed our tests! We each had our first ice skating badge. Jill looked really happy and said she was very proud of us. Mother just kept smiling.

Then Jill did something special. She showed us some of the things we could hope to do if we worked hard. Jill did spins and jumps and spirals. She blended her moves together and they looked very graceful. Lewis and I smiled at each other. We could hardly wait to start new ice skating classes!

Words about ICE SKATING

BACKWARD SWIZZLE: A backward move tracing opposing curves with both feet on the ice

COMPULSORY FIGURES: That part of figure skating in which the skaters do certain moves based on the figure eight

EDGE: One of the two sides of the bottom of a skate blade, formed by the groove that runs the length of the blade. Edges are important for controlling direction.

FIGURE EIGHT: Two circles on the ice that almost touch. To skate a figure eight a skater skates around one circle on one foot and then skates the other circle on the other foot. Advanced skaters also learn one-foot figure eights and figures that have three circles.

FORWARD CROSSOVER: A way of changing from one foot to the other while skating in a circle or around a curve. The skate on the outside of the curve is crossed around the front of the inside skate. This is frequently used for gaining speed on curves.

FORWARD STROKING: Skating forward by pushing off against the inside of the back blade and gliding on the forward blade

FREE FOOT: That foot not in contact with the ice

FREESTYLE: The part of figure skating that allows skaters to combine jumps, spins, steps, and spirals any way they like in a program set to music

GLIDE: The movement forward or backward on skate blades

INSIDE EDGE: The edge of the skate blade that runs along the big-toe side of the foot

OUTSIDE EDGE: The edge of the skate blade that runs along the small-toe side of the foot

PATCH: An area of ice rented by a skater to practice figures

PROGRAM: A skater's sequence of steps, spins, spirals, and other moves. They are set to music and skated for a certain period of time.

PUSH OFF: To thrust forward or backward by pushing against the ice with a blade edge

SKATE GUARDS: Protectors for skate blades so they won't become dull if a skater walks on surfaces other than ice.

SKATING FOOT: The foot that is in contact with the ice

SNOWPLOW STOP: A stop that can be done using one foot or both feet. In a two-foot snowplow stop, both toes are turned in, both knees are bent, and the skater skids to a stop.

TOE PICKS: The teeth at the front of figure-skate blades. They are used for making certain jumps, spins, and other skating moves. They are sometimes used for stopping, but only with certain movements.

ABOUT THE AUTHORS

LOWELL A. DICKMEYER is active in athletics as a participant, instructor, and writer. He is particularly interested in youth sport programs, and each summer he organizes sports camps for hundreds of youngsters. Mr. Dickmeyer has been a college physical education instructor and an elementary school principal in southern California.

LIN ROLENS teaches creative writing at Ventura College in southern California and is also a freelance writer and book reviewer for the *Los Angeles Times*. She enjoys skating and jogging and has escorted children on tennis trips to England.

ABOUT THE PHOTOGRAPHER

ALAN ODDIE was born and raised in Scotland. He now resides in Santa Monica, California. In addition to his work as a photographer, Mr. Oddie is an author and a producer of educational filmstrips. He is currently the staff photographer for *Franciscan Communications*.

Ron Priestley
Editorial Consultant

DATE DUE